MY LiTTLE HALf-MOON

WRITTEN BY DOUGLAS TODD JENNERICH

ILLUSTRATED BY KATE BERUBE

G. P. PUTNAM'S SONS

One night I looked up at half of the moon,
And I hoped to myself that the other half soon
Would please stop its hiding and come out to play.
I hoped myself into the very next day.

And when daytime got sleepy and nighttime woke up,
I made some hot cocoa and filled up my cup.
I went to the yard and looked at the sky
To see if the moon's other half had arrived.

Sadly, it hadn't, and a thought came to me:
How lonely a half of a moon he must be!
No one to glow with and everyone knowing
How sad is the face that the half a moon's showing.

No one to play with and no one to share
How much he likes puppies and big, fuzzy bears.
How much he likes ice cream and chocolate and pie,
Which is funny because, don't you know, so do I!

From that moment on, I decided to stay
Every night with the moon and a PB&J
Till the sun came back up and the stars went away
And my little half-moon was a moon all the way.

That was my plan, and I did it with ease—
I stood there and stared at that big piece of cheese.
Me on the grass and him in the sky,
But he never got brighter, and I didn't know why.

Night after night, for what seemed like a year,
I watched for the moon's other half to appear.

To cheer up the moon, I brought different things,
But he wasn't impressed with the things I would bring.

I showed him my fire truck,
showed him my bike

And anything else that I thought he might like.

A kitten, a cricket, a frog with a tail,
A lizard, a beetle, a slug and a snail.

I brought him a pencil, a crayon, some chalk.
Do you think the moon noticed? Not even a balk!

I brought him an ostrich wearing a sweater
And said he could look, but he better not pet her—
They bite and they kick and they get so unfettered,
I was risking my life and my limbs just to get her!

Then I got mad, what else could I do?

"Moon, what's the matter? I'm talking to you!
I brought you a lolly, a purple kazoo,
A peacock, a pumpkin, a bamboo canoe,
A marshmallow dripping in chocolate fondue . . .

But you're still just a half of a moon in the sky—
Hey, I'm talking to you! I want to know why!"

And right at that moment, I noticed a trace
Of brightness appear on the moon's half a face.
Could it be? Was it crazy? Was I possibly heard,
And the moon was responding to my every word?

People like talking, so why not the moon?
I gave him attention from midnight till noon.
I read him some books and reminded him how
Important he was to the bats and the owls,
The wind and the seas and the seasons and trees,
And oh, how important to little old me!

I told him without him, the world would be dim,
How tides in the ocean were all 'cause of him,
How he keeps the night safe for the fawns and the fowl,
That he was the reason that dogs and wolves howl.

Then one night, I woke up to tell him again.

I walked out and looked
and my heart leapt up when

The whole sky was bright, and astounded I found
My shadow was twenty feet long on the ground!

The moon he was glowing, so cheerful and yellow,
I've not in my life seen a happier fellow!
He hung there so big and perfectly round,
Displaying the bright other half he had found.

It worked! I had done it! It just took some talking!
I stopped and I chatted, rather than walking
When I'd seen that my moon hadn't been quite
As whole as he could be, and not quite as bright.

So at least in my yard, and at least on this night,
You'd think it was noon, the night sky was so bright.
The moon stopped its hiding to come out to play,
And if you ask me, it's better that way.

When something's in half, I will help find the rest,
For a half-moon is nice, but a full moon's the best.